Beautiful Buehla
and the Zany Zoo Makeover

GARY HOGG 🐾 Illustrated by VICTORIA CHESS

KATHERINE TEGEN BOOKS
An Imprint of HarperCollins *Publishers*

Library of Congress Cataloging-in-Publication Data
Hogg, Gary, 1953-
  Beautiful Buehla / Gary Hogg ; illustrated by Victoria Chess.— 1st ed.
    p. cm.
  Summary: Buehla, of Beautiful Buehla's Beauty Parlor, tries to get the zoo
animals ready to have their picture taken.
  ISBN-13: 978-0-06-009420-1 (trade bdg.)
  ISBN-10: 0-06-009420-6 (trade bdg.)
  ISBN-13: 978-0-06-009421-8 (lib. bdg.)
  ISBN-10: 0-06-009421-4 (lib. bdg.)
  [1. Beauty, Personal—Fiction. 2. Zoo animals—Fiction. 3. Photographs—
Fiction.] I. Chess, Victoria, ill. II. Title.
PZ7.H68353Bea 2006   2005015162
[E]—dc22   CIP
                                                              AC

Typography by Jeanne L. Hogle
1 2 3 4 5 6 7 8 9 10
❖

For my beautiful mother —G.H.

$\mathcal{M}$r. Phibbs, the zookeeper, was in a panic. It was picture day at the zoo, and the animals weren't ready.

"I need help," said the zookeeper, opening the phone book. He turned to the advertisement for Beautiful Buehla's Beauty Parlor: "Are you a mess? Don't know what to do? Beautiful Buehla can make a BEAUTIFUL you!"

Perfect! thought Mr. Phibbs.

"Hello, it's a beautiful day!"

sang Buehla into the phone.

The zookeeper began to explain his prob—

"Say no more," Buehla cut in. "Be there in a flash."

Beautiful Buehla grabbed her beauty-to-go bag and raced to the zoo.

"You must be Buehla," said Mr. Phibbs.

"Just call me Beautiful," said Buehla.

She gave the zoo a professional once-over. "These animals are a mess to the max!"

"Oh my," said Mr. Phibbs. "The photographer will be here soon."

"You need a miracle," she added.

"Oh no!" cried poor Mr. Phibbs. "Where can I find a miracle at this hour?"

"Dum da da dum!" trumpeted Buehla. "I'll beautify this bunch in no time."

"Whew," sighed the zookeeper. "Can I get you anything?" he asked.

Beautiful Buehla searched her supplies. "Face powder," she boomed.

Mr. Phibbs scuttled off.

Buehla turned and caught sight of the lion's shaggy mane.
"Frizzies!" she squealed.

With a roar, the hungry lion bared his sharp teeth.

"I like an enthusiastic customer," said Buehla. And then—
POW! Buehla's hands flew into a frenzy, working one tool
after another. She combed and cut and curled and teased the
lion's mane into a swirling heap of hair.

"Beautiful!" bellowed Buehla.
"One more can of hair spray and you'll be perfect."

The lion wasn't so sure.

"Yoo-hoo," called Buehla to the hippo.

The hippo wiggled her ears and trudged ashore.

Buehla shook her head sadly. "Oh, honey, you've really let yourself go.

"Now. Rocket-Red lipstick—It's you! Lizard Belly Green Eye Shadow—All the rage! Downright Purple Plum Rouge—Sensational!

"Beautiful!" bellowed Buehla, holding up a mirror. "The 'hip' is back in the 'hippo.'"

The hippo's mouth dropped.

"Don't worry about your makeup," said Buehla. "It's waterproof."

Buehla found Bing and Bob hiding behind a log.

"Typical boys," Buehla said, and sighed. "Afraid of a little fashion."

She eyed the bears.

Bing scratched his back. Bob licked his paws.

"Dancers!" cried Buehla. "So natural, too. I always keep emergency disco outfits in the Beautymobile.

"Beautiful!" bellowed Buehla.

"Disco dudes!"

Buehla began to boogie. She boogied around the trees. She boogied through the flowers. She boogied down the path until—

WHAM! She was face-to-face with Large Marge.

Large Marge blinked.

"Sweetheart, a pretty girl like you needs luscious lashes to flutter," said Buehla. "Don't worry, I picked up some extendo-lashes on the way over.

"Beautiful!" bellowed Buehla. "The camera is going to love you."

Large Marge lumbered off, tail swishing.

Mr. Phibbs's exotic snake collection was resting peacefully—until Buehla crashed through the door.

"Rise and shine! Rise and shine!" she called out.

With a shrill blast from her whistle, Buehla began the workout.

Hut – Two – Three – Four,
Lazy snakes are a bore.
Five – Six – Seven – Eight,
Stay in bed and get up late.
Hut – Two – Three – Four,
Peppy snakes know the score.
Five – Six – Seven – Eight,
They stay lean and stand up straight!

"*Beautiful!*" bellowed Buehla, inspecting the troops.

"Photo op at o-sixteen-hundred," she barked. "Remember: tongues in and chests out."

The gorilla was in no mood for beauty.

"Oh dear," said Buehla. "I can't beautify through that negative energy."

She unrolled her yoga mat. Her chanting soothed the savage beast.

"What to do? What to do?" said Buehla.

Inspiration hit—PINK!

"My personal favorite, and a crowd-pleaser to boot.

"Beautiful!" bellowed Buehla. "I love it!"

The gorilla awoke with a start. Pink was not his favorite color.

"Here comes the photographer now," said Buehla.

"I am Señor Pablo Martinez," the photographer said grandly.

"Just call me Beautiful," said Buehla, extending her hand.

The photographer set up his equipment while Beautiful Buehla bossed the animals into position.

Mr. Phibbs came scuttling up the path.

"Ta-dah!" Buehla exulted.

"But, but, but . . ." stammered Mr. Phibbs.

"Speechless with joy," said Buehla, beaming. "That's beauty for you."
"I'm not so sure about this," said Mr. Phibbs.

"Ready," Señor Martinez called. "But Beautiful must be in the picture too."

"Me?" Beautiful Buehla blushed, pushing her way to the front.

"My face powder," she roared. "Phibbs, where is it?"

Buehla's puff sent powder billowing into the air.

Large Marge broke her pose. First her tail began to switch. Then she began to twitch. And to itch. She switched, and twitched, and itched until—

AHH-CHOO!

It was a world-record blast!

"How do we look?" prompted Beautiful Buehla.

"*Beautiful!*" bellowed Mr. Phibbs as Señor Martinez snapped the picture.

SAFARI TATTLER

ZOO BEAUTIFUL

Picture day at the zoo presented a problem for its director, Mr. Phibbs. The animals were in need of a makeover, and so Mr. Phibbs called in a beauty expert, Beautiful Buehla, to work her magic. Makeovers are extremely popular these days, and Mr. Phibbs thought the animals would welcome their transformations.

Some of the animals weren't convinced that a makeover was what they needed. It is often the case that natural beauty supersedes the kind of packaging that our popular culture seems to expect. Picture day ended in a satisfactory manner, however, when Large Marge the elephant adjusted some of Buehla's efforts.

Beautiful Buehla's Beauty Parlor:
Are you a mess? Don't know what to do?
Beautiful Buehla can make a beautiful you!

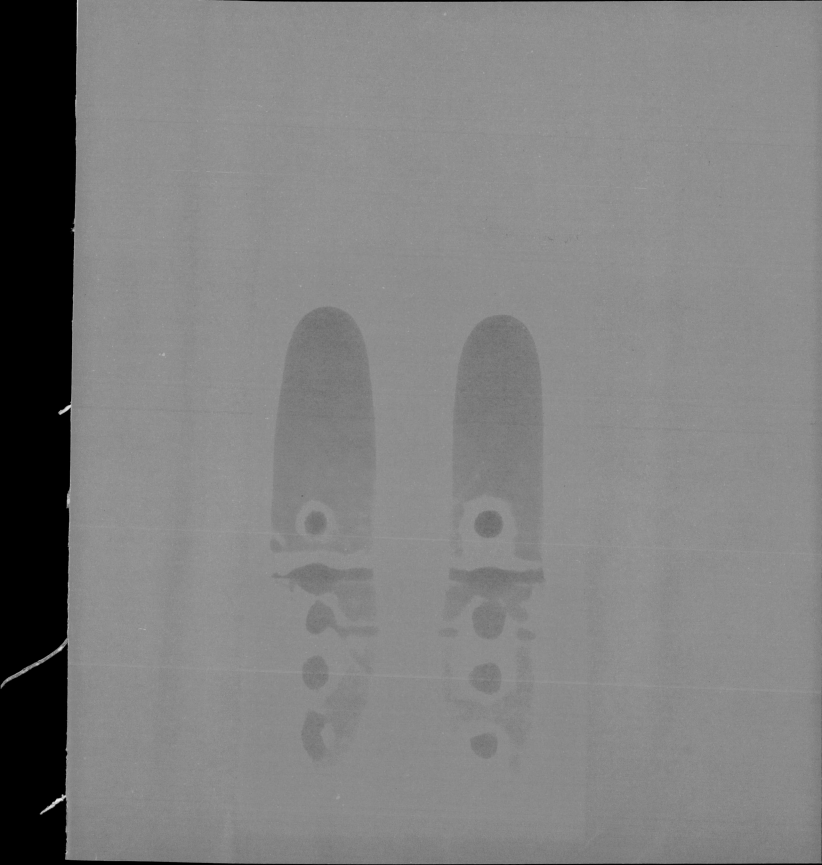